Blast Off

By Susie Piper

NUTMEG

SUGAR

Pioneer Valley Educational Press, Inc.

One day Sugar said,
"Look! Let's play in this big box!"

Nutmeg jumped up
and looked into the box.
"What can we play?" she asked.

"I have an idea," said Sugar.
"It can be a spaceship."

Sugar and Nutmeg jumped
into the box. They looked all around.

"We are in a spaceship!" said Sugar.

"Where are we going?" asked Nutmeg.

"Let's go to the moon," said Sugar.

"Good idea!" Nutmeg said.
"The moon is made of cheese!
I love cheese!"

Sugar and Nutmeg
began to count down.

"Five!

    Four!

        Three!

            Two!

                One!

Blast off!" they shouted.

9

Nutmeg looked over the top
of the box.
"Look! We're going up!" she said.

"We're blasting off!" said Sugar.

"Oh! Oh!" cried Nutmeg.
"Look Sugar! We **are** going up!"

11

Then Sugar looked over the top of the box. "Yikes!" cried Sugar. "We **are** blasting off!"